MISS BROWNE

MISS BROWNE

The Story of a Superior Mouse

Illustrated by
MADELINE HALL

Hart Publishing Company, Inc. • New York City

7084

MISS BROWNE

Dear Mrs. Grey, at Sweet Briar Farm
   Got a letter which came from the town;
It was written to say, to expect the next day,
   Her cousin, the fancy Miss Browne.

Mrs. Grey and her daughters, took brooms and took waters
　　To make their house tidy and clean.
They worried and hurried; they scrubbed and they scurried
　　Till the room was fit for a queen.

Miss Browne was a lady of elegant style;
   She lived in a church in the town.
On her cousins, the Greys, with their quaint country ways—
   Miss Browne was inclined to look down.

11

Miss Browne arrived just in time for lunch:
   There were biscuits and corn piled in dishes,
And pastry and milk, and cheese smooth as silk—
   The food was really delicious!

13

Miss Browne talked much of her elegant home,
And of what *she* was used to eat:
"We never eat cheese, and such dishes as these!"
Mrs. Grey blushed right down to her feet!

15

"We nibble on velvet and genuine oak,
   On cassocks and prayer books and rice,
On old ladies' fans, and fruits out of cans—
   And the jellies are so very nice!"

The cats from next door, heard her boasts and grew sore;
  They resented her uppity way.
They listened and purred—to them all it occurred
  That Miss Browne would be easy prey.

19

Miss Browne rattled on, unaware that the others
  Were fleeing the table in haste!
"We don't fear a cat, and a trap is old hat."
  She knew not the danger she faced.

Then before she could say—"I am lost! Woe the day!"
  She was seized by a powerful Tom.
All her boasts and her scorn, and her finery worn,
  Couldn't save that proud lady from harm.

23

Her cousins the Greys, were wise to cats' ways,
And sensed they were out on the prowl.
But Miss Browne, the proud, kept talking so loud,
She fell victim to murder most foul.